JUNIOR BIOS

Billie Eilish

BY NORA GARDINER

Enslow PUBLISHING

Please visit our website, www.enslow.com. For a free color catalog of all our high-quality books, call toll free 1-800-398-2504 or fax 1-877-980-4454.

Library of Congress Cataloging-in-Publication Data

Names: Gardiner, Nora, author.
Title: Billie Eilish / Nora Gardiner.
Description: New York : Enslow Publishing, 2022. | Series: Junior bios | Includes index.
Identifiers: LCCN 2020033824 | ISBN 9781978522640 (library binding) | ISBN 9781978522626 (paperback) | ISBN 9781978522633 (6 pack) | ISBN 9781978522657 (ebook)
Subjects: LCSH: Eilish, Billie, 2001—Juvenile literature. | Singers—United States—Biography—Juvenile literature.
Classification: LCC ML3930.E35 G37 2022 | DDC 782.42164092—dc23
LC record available at https://lccn.loc.gov/2020033824

First Edition

Published in 2022 by
Enslow Publishing
29 E. 21st Street
New York, NY 10010

Designer: Deanna Paternostro
Editor: Kate Mikoley

Photo credits: Cover, p. 1 (Billie Eilish) David M. Benett/Contributor/Getty Images Entertainment/Getty Images; cover, p. 1 (photo frame) Aleksandr Andrushkiv/Shutterstock.com; marble texture used throughout Hardtllustrations/Shutterstock.com; lined paper texture used throughout Mtsaride/Shutterstock.com; watercolor texture used throughout solarbird/Shutterstock.com; p. 5 Karwai Tang/Contributor/WireImage/Getty Images; p. 7 Jeff Kravitz/Contributor/FilmMagic, Inc./Getty Images; p. 9 PYMCA/Contributor/Universal Images Group/Getty Images; p. 11 Frank Hoensch/Contributor/Redferns/Getty Images; p. 13 Kevin Winter/Staff/Getty Images Entertainment/Getty Images; p. 15 Kevin Mazur/Contributor/Getty Images Entertainment/Getty Images; p. 17 Alberto E. Rodriguez/Stringer/Getty Images Entertainment/Getty Images; p. 19 Gregg DeGuire/Stringer/WireImage/Getty Images.

Printed in the United States of America

CPSIA compliance information: Batch #CSENS22: For further information contact Enslow Publishing, New York, New York, at 1-800-398-2504.

Contents

Words in the glossary appear in **bold** type the first time they are used in the text.

All About Billie

At 17, a lot of people spend their time going to class, thinking about what they'll do after high school, and perhaps learning to drive or working an after-school job. When Billie Eilish was 17, she was celebrating her first number one album. Not long after turning 18, she won some of music's biggest awards.

Billie shot to fame when she uploaded a song to the music-sharing website SoundCloud at just 14 years old. The song, "Ocean Eyes," quickly became a hit. Fast forward a few years, and Billie is one of the biggest pop stars on the planet!

AFTER BILLIE POSTED "OCEAN EYES" ON SOUNDCLOUD, THE SONG WENT VIRAL. THIS MEANS IT SPREAD QUICKLY THROUGH THE INTERNET.

Talent in the Family

Billie was born on December 18, 2001. Her full name is Billie Eilish Pirate Baird O'Connell. Her parents, Maggie Baird and Patrick O'Connell, named her after Maggie's father, Bill, who died before Billie was born. When Billie became famous, she decided to use her first and middle name as her stage name.

FACTS BEHIND THE FIGURE

Billie's older brother, Finneas, was four when she was born. He wanted to call her "Pirate." Her parents had other plans for her name, but the nickname stuck around as a second middle name.

FINNEAS OFTEN PLAYS ONSTAGE WITH BILLIE DURING HER SHOWS. HE HAS ALSO RELEASED, OR COME OUT WITH, SOME OF HIS OWN MUSIC.

Billie is close with her older brother, Finneas. They even work together! Finneas produces and helps write Billie's music. In fact, Finneas wrote Billie's first hit, "Ocean Eyes." The song was originally meant to be given to Billie's dance teacher to create a dance to.

Singing Since the Beginning

Billie has been singing for as long as she can remember. When she was 8, she joined the Los Angeles Children's **Chorus**. The group helped her learn important skills for singing. By the time she was about 11, she was already writing her own songs.

FACTS BEHIND THE FIGURE

Even though Billie never went to a **traditional** school, she graduated high school at 15! She did this by taking and passing a test that showed she knew enough to finish school.

BETWEEN BEING IN THE CHORUS AND DANCING, BILLIE WAS ALREADY USED TO PERFORMING BY THE TIME SHE BECAME FAMOUS.

Lots of young stars struggle with balancing work and the rest of their lives. For Billie, one thing that helped was that she'd always been homeschooled. When she became famous, she was able to continue with school this way. It meant she could find time to learn between concerts, recording, and other responsibilities.

When "Ocean Eyes" went viral on SoundCloud, Billie caught the attention of not just new fans but also professionals in the music **industry**. A record company signed her, and the song was officially put out as her **debut** single, or song, in November 2016.

In Her Own Words

"I hope [my music] will inspire people to try to **achieve** their goals, no matter how difficult they might be. I didn't think I would get anywhere but I did because I worked hard and really believed in myself."

SOON AFTER HER EP CAME OUT, BILLIE SET OUT ON HER FIRST-EVER TOUR. SHE PLAYED SHOWS AROUND NORTH AMERICA, FROM CALIFORNIA TO CANADA.

In August 2017, Billie came out with her first EP, called *Don't Smile at Me*. "EP" stands for "extended play." An EP is a music album that has fewer songs than a full-length album. *Don't Smile at Me* included "Ocean Eyes," as well as seven other songs. In December 2017, it was rereleased with an additional song.

TV Tunes

In 2017, Billie's song "Bored" was featured on the popular Netflix show *13 Reasons Why*. The following year, another of her songs was included in the show's second season. This song, "Lovely," was a **collaboration** with fellow musician Khalid.

FACTS BEHIND THE FIGURE

Billie has performed on several late-night TV shows. In 2019, she got one of the biggest TV opportunities available for musicians—she was the musical guest on *Saturday Night Live*, a popular late-night **comedy** show.

BILLIE AND KHALID'S SONG "LOVELY" WAS RANKED AT THE TOP OF A LIST OF MOST POPULAR SONGS ON TV SHOWS FOR MAY 2018.

Other shows Billie's songs have been featured on include *Pretty Little Liars* and *The Vampire Diaries*. Her song "Six Feet Under" was used in a trailer for the popular show *American Horror Story* in 2019.

Billie's songs have been in movies too. "Ocean Eyes" was featured on the **soundtracks** for the movies *Everything, Everything* (2017) and *The Hate U Give* (2018).

Hitting the Charts

In 2018, Billie came out with several more singles. In 2019, she released her first full-length album, titled *When We All Fall Asleep, Where Do We Go?* The week the album came out, Billie had 14 songs on the Billboard Hot 100 chart. This is a chart put out by *Billboard* magazine, used as a standard in the music industry for ranking songs.

FACTS BEHIND THE FIGURE

While Billie's new music was coming out, she also kept performing regularly. In 2019, she performed at Coachella, a well-known music festival in California.

WITH 14 SONGS ON THE HOT 100 CHART, BILLIE SET A RECORD FOR THE MOST SONGS ANY FEMALE ARTIST EVER HAD ON THE CHART AT ONCE.

The album itself came out at number one on the Billboard 200, a list used to rank entire albums. This feat made Billie the first artist born in the 2000s to have a number one album.

Sweeping the Grammys

Each year, the Grammy Awards honor many of the year's biggest stars in music. Winning a Grammy is a huge achievement for any musician. For someone new in the industry, it can mean an even bigger push to fame.

FACTS BEHIND THE FIGURE

When Billie won the Grammys for Album and Record of the Year, she became the youngest person to ever win in these categories.

WHEN SOMEONE WINS ALL FOUR OF THE BIG AWARDS, IT'S CALLED A SWEEP. BILLIE WAS ONLY THE SECOND PERSON EVER TO DO THIS!

The four biggest awards at the Grammys are Best New Artist, Record of the Year, Song of the Year, and Album of the Year. In 2020, Billie won all four of these, plus one more award for Best Pop Vocal Album. She also performed during the show, alongside her brother, Finneas, who shared in several of her awards and won two of his own.

Keeping It Real

In 2018, Billie stated that she has Tourette syndrome, a condition that causes a person to move or talk in a way they can't control. After opening up about her experience, Billie said many of her fans revealed their own experiences with Tourette syndrome. She said this made her feel a connection with the fans.

In Her Own Words

"What's the point of pleasing other people? You've got to get out and change the world, and we're the ***generation*** *that's going to step into that."*

BILLIE HAS TALKED ABOUT THE IMPORTANCE OF BEING YOURSELF AND NOT WORRYING ABOUT WHAT OTHER PEOPLE THINK. PERHAPS THAT ATTITUDE IS WHY HER MUSIC IS SO UNIQUE!

Much of Billie's music has a dark or even creepy sound. She's said that some of her inspiration comes from bad dreams and night terrors, or episodes similar to but more dramatic than nightmares. These scary events helped her create *When We All Fall Asleep, Where Do We Go?*

Busy Times for Billie

Billie doesn't take her success for granted. She makes time for meet-and-greets with fans and speaks out about issues close to her, such as mental health and caring for the environment. She's a busy star, but Billie enjoys spending her downtime with her family and friends. She also likes horses. When she was younger, she worked at a stable to pay for riding lessons.

From Grammys to world tours, Billie Eilish has certainly accomplished a lot—especially for such a young musician. With a long future ahead of her, it's anyone's guess what's in store next for this superstar!

Billie's Timeline

DECEMBER 18, 2001: BILLIE IS BORN.

NOVEMBER 2015: BILLIE AND FINNEAS UPLOAD "OCEAN EYES" TO SOUNDCLOUD.

NOVEMBER 2016: "OCEAN EYES" IS OFFICIALLY RELEASED AS BILLIE'S FIRST SINGLE.

AUGUST 2017: BILLIE'S FIRST EP, *DON'T SMILE AT ME*, COMES OUT.

OCTOBER 2017: BILLIE BEGINS HER FIRST TOUR.

MARCH 2019: *WHEN WE ALL FALL ASLEEP, WHERE DO WE GO?* IS RELEASED.

SEPTEMBER 2019: BILLIE IS THE MUSICAL GUEST ON *SATURDAY NIGHT LIVE*.

JANUARY 2020: BILLIE SWEEPS THE GRAMMYS, WINNING A TOTAL OF FIVE AWARDS.

Glossary

achieve To get or reach something, such as a goal, by working hard.

chorus A large group of singers.

collaboration A work produced by two or more people working together.

comedy A work meant to make people laugh.

debut A first appearance or release.

generation A group of individuals born about the same time.

industry A group of businesses or people providing a similar service.

soundtrack The music used in a movie.

traditional Based on what is considered typical or normal.

For More Information

Books

Morgan, Sally. *Billie Eilish: The Ultimate Unofficial Fanbook*. New York, NY: Scholastic Inc., 2019.

Wills, Amy. *Billie Eilish: Your Unofficial Guide to the Most Talked About Teen on the Planet* (Idols of Pop). New York, NY: HarperCollins, 2020.

Websites

All Things Billie Eilish
www.kidzworld.com/article/31472-all-things-billie-eilish/
Find out more about Billie here.

Billie Eilish
www.billieeilish.com/
Check out Billie's official website for all the latest news about the pop star's music.

Publisher's note to educators and parents: Our editors have carefully reviewed these websites to ensure that they are suitable for students. Many websites change frequently, however, and we cannot guarantee that a site's future contents will continue to meet our high standards of quality and educational value. Be advised that students should be closely supervised whenever they access the internet.

Index